SCAB

by Rachel Rose

Consultant: Beth Gambro
Reading Specialist, Yorkville, Illinois

BEARPORT
PUBLISHING

Minneapolis, Minnesota

Teaching Tips

Before Reading

- Look at the cover of the book. Discuss the picture and the title.

- Ask readers to brainstorm a list of what they already know about scabs. What can they expect to see in this book?

- Go on a picture walk, looking through the pictures to discuss vocabulary and make predictions about the text.

During Reading

- Read for purpose. Encourage readers to think about scabs as they are reading.

- Ask readers to look for the details of the book. What are they learning about the body and how it forms scabs?

- If readers encounter an unknown word, ask them to look at the sounds in the word. Then, ask them to look at the rest of the page. Are there any clues to help them understand?

After Reading

- Encourage readers to pick a buddy and reread the book together.

- Ask readers to explain what happens under a scab. Find the page that tells about this.

- Ask readers to write or draw something they learned about scabs.

Credits: Cover and title page, © RubberBall/Alamy; 3, © BartCo/iStock; 5, © miljko/iStock; 6–7, © dilyaz/Shutterstock; 9, © NatchaS/iStock; 11, © Image Source/Getty Images; 13, © yacobchuk/iStock; 15, © MagicBones/Shutterstock; 18–19, © Makhh/Shutterstock and © Roman Samborskyi/Shutterstock; 21, © antoniodiaz/Shutterstock; 22L, © gritsalak karalak/Shutterstock; 22R, © Tetiana Lazunova/iStock; 23TL, © toeytoey2530/iStock; 23TC, © Raycat/iStock; 23TR, © Jelena Stanojkovic/iStock; 23BL, © kokoroyuki/iStock; 23BC, © Douglas Rissing/iStock; and 23BR, © Ermolaeva Olga 84/Shutterstock.

Library of Congress Cataloging-in-Publication Data is available at www.loc.gov or upon request from the publisher.

ISBN: 979-8-88509-338-5 (hardcover)
ISBN: 979-8-88509-460-3 (paperback)
ISBN: 979-8-88509-575-4 (ebook)

For more information, write to Bearport Publishing, 5357 Penn Avenue South, Minneapolis, MN 55419.

Contents

A Bloody Knee

Yesterday, I fell off my bike and cut my knee.

Ouch!

Now, I have a **scab**.

Why does my body do that?

Scabs help your skin **heal**.

Everyone gets them.

But how do scabs form?

They start when you bleed from a cut.

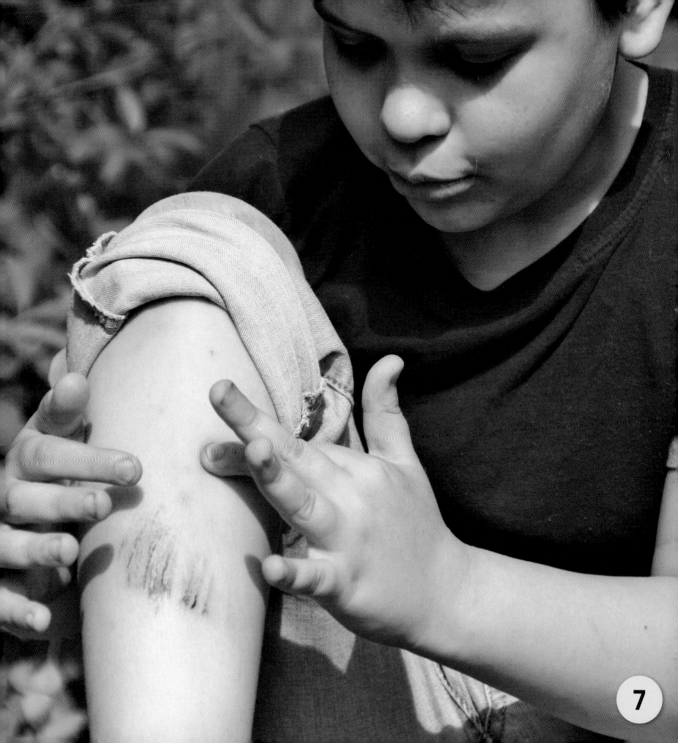

Your blood is made of tiny **cells**.

When you bleed, some cells stick together.

They cover your cut to stop the bleeding.

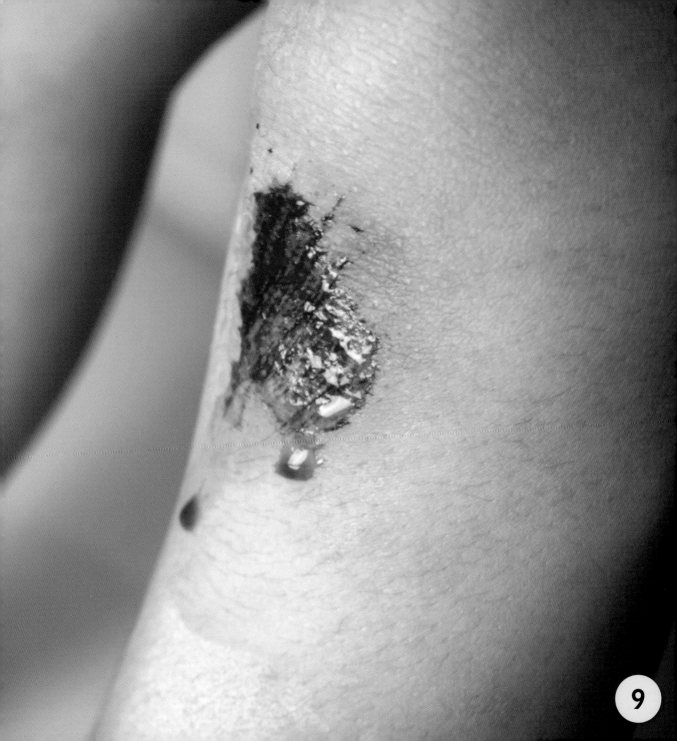

When the sticky blood cells dry, they become hard.

This is a scab.

It may be brown or red.

What does a scab do?

It stops **germs** from getting into the cut.

This keeps your body healthy.

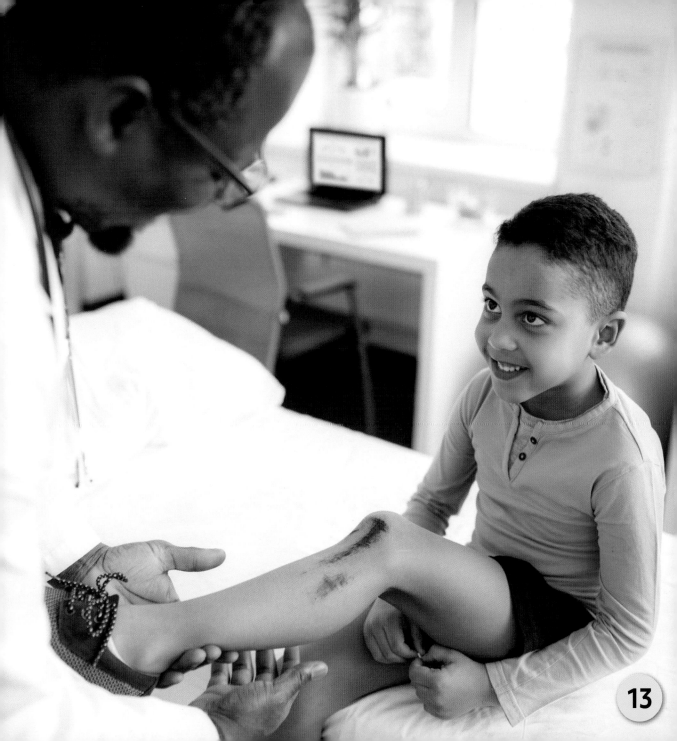

Something happens under the scab, too.

Your body is hard at work.

It is making new skin!

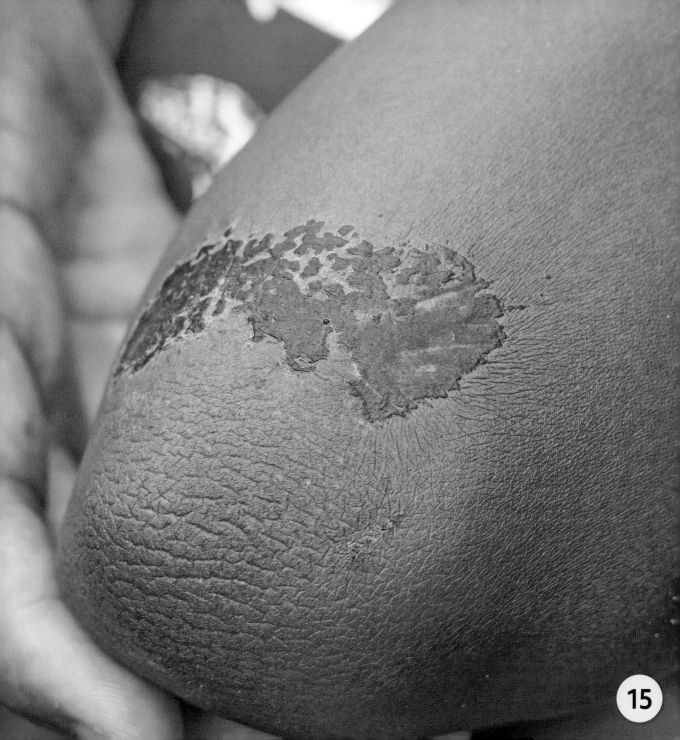

Sometimes, a scab may feel **itchy**.

Try not to **scratch** it.

That will slow down the healing.

Covering the scab with a bandage can help.

After a while, the scab will fall off.

There may be a small mark left behind.

But usually, your skin will look the same as before.

It is never fun to get a cut. But having a scab is good. It means your body is healing. Your skin will be like new!

See It Happen

When you get a cut, you start to bleed.

Cells in the blood stick together. They form a scab.

Your body makes new skin under the scab.

Then, the scab falls off.

Glossary

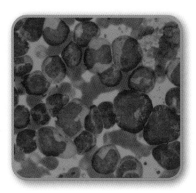

cells the tiny parts of all living things

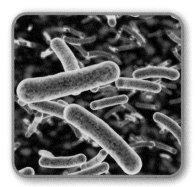

germs tiny living things that can make people sick

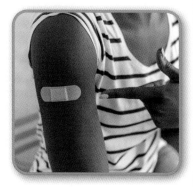

heal to become healthy again

itchy a tickly feeling that makes you want to scratch

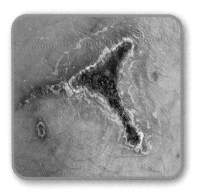

scab dry blood that covers a cut

scratch to rub or scrape at something

Index

Read More

Brundle, Joanna. *Cuts and Bleeding (My First Aid Guide to . . .).* New York: Kidhaven Publishing, 2022.

Dufresne, Emilie. *Human Body Facts (Fact-o-graphics!).* Minneapolis: Bearport Publishing, 2022.

Learn More Online

1. Go to **www.factsurfer.com** or scan the QR code below.
2. Enter "**Scab**" into the search box.
3. Click on the cover of this book to see a list of websites.

About the Author

Rachel Rose lives in California. She thinks the body is amazing with all its superpowers, like making scabs to heal!